# PUFFIN BOOKS

## The Fwog Prince the twuth!

Kaye Umansky was born in Plymouth, Devon. Her favourite books as a child were the *Just William* books, *Alice in Wonderland*, *The Hobbit* and *The Swish of the Curtain*. She went to Teacher's Training College, after which she taught in London primary schools for twelve years, specialising in music and drama. In her spare time she sang and played keyboards with a semiprofessional soul band.

She now writes full time – or as full time as she can get in between trips to Sainsbury's and looking after her husband (Mo), daughter (Ella, aged ten) and cats (Charlie and Alfie).

*Other books by Kaye Umansky*

PONGWIFFY
PONGWIFFY AND THE GOBLINS' REVENGE
PONGWIFFY AND THE SPELL OF THE YEAR
PONGWIFFY AND THE HOLIDAY OF DOOM

*Non-fiction*

DO NOT OPEN BEFORE CHRISTMAS DAY!
WITCHES IN STITCHES

*For younger readers*

KING KEITH AND THE JOLLY LODGER
THE ROMANTIC GIANT

# Kaye Umansky

# The
# Fwog Prince
## the twuth!

*Illustrated by Gwyneth Williamson*

PUFFIN BOOKS

PUFFIN BOOKS

Published by the Penguin Group
Penguin Books Ltd, 27 Wrights Lane, London W8 5TZ, England
Penguin Books USA Inc., 375 Hudson Street, New York, New York 10014, USA
Penguin Books Australia Ltd, Ringwood, Victoria, Australia
Penguin Books Canada Ltd, 10 Alcorn Avenue, Toronto, Ontario, Canada M4V 3B2
Penguin Books (NZ) Ltd, 182–190 Wairau Road, Auckland 10, New Zealand

Penguin Books Ltd, Registered Offices: Harmondsworth, Middlesex, England

First published by A & C Black (Publishers) Ltd 1989
Published in Puffin Books 1991
1 3 5 7 9 10 8 6 4 2

Filmset in Monotype Plantin

Made and printed in England by Clays Ltd, St Ives plc

# What do you think?

You probably know the story of the Frog Prince. It goes like this: an obviously spoilt Princess drops her golden ball into a well and makes a great fuss about it. A talking frog appears (eh?) and fetches the ball. The obviously spoilt Princess is hateful to him (boo!). It turns out that he is a handsome Prince (surprise, surprise), who has been transformed by a wicked Witch (why?). Then they get married (why?).

Have you ever wondered about all this? Like, why play with an expensive golden ball when an old tennis ball would do? What's it like being a frog? Was the Princess surprised to meet a talking frog? Would *you* be? Why did she break her promise? What had he done to be changed into a frog in the first place? Who was the Witch concerned? Did the Prince have a history of being changed into a frog, or was it a one-off occurrence? Would he really marry the Princess after she'd been so nasty to him? Would *she* marry *him* in view of his shady past? What do you think?

WARNING!
THERE IS NOBODY NICE
IN THIS STORY AT ALL!

# CHAPTER ONE

# In Which We Meet Prince Pipsqueak

'Once upon a time, there was a handsome young Prince who had the misfortune to offend a wicked Witch. In order to avenge herself, the Witch cast a spell over the Prince, turning him into an ugly frog.'

Well now. Let's get the facts straight. Prince Pipsqueak certainly wasn't handsome. Oh, he was a Prince all right. You could tell that at a glance. At least, you could before he got turned into a frog. After that, of course, it was a bit more difficult.

Here is Prince Pipsqueak before.

And here he is after.

You have to admit that the Witch did a thorough job.

Take a good look at the 'before' Pipsqueak. Note the princely trappings. Castle with attached moat. Crown, horse, coach, servants, smart clothes, room of his own, far too much pocket money and ridiculously expensive shoes.

Of course, if you took all that away, he would seem perfectly ordinary. Until he opened his mouth, that is. When he did that, he used A Certain Tone Of Voice – and you could tell right away that he wasn't normal.

Oooh. That Tone Of Voice. It was bold, brash and bossy. It was snooty, snobby and sneery. It was haughty, high-handed and hoity-toity. It cut through conversations like a hedge-trimmer cuts through privet.

'I Say! Peasant! Thwow down your cloak, I the Pwince wish to cwoss over this puddle!'

'You there! Waiter! This cup is cwacked. Don't you know I'm the Pwince?'

'Take me to the palace, cabby, and look sharp about it! What d'you mean *pay* you? I'm the Pwince!'

'I don't believe it! I simply don't *believe* it!! I'm the Pwince, and nobody's fluffed up my *thwone* cushion again!'

See what I mean? Let's face it. Prince Pipsqueak had a way of saying things that was guaranteed to get people's backs up. It got waiters' backs up. It got cab drivers' backs up. It got the servants' backs up. It even got his mother's back up (his mother, of course, being the Queen. Queen Mona).

'Pipsqueak, I *do* wish you would talk to Pipsqueak Junior,' the Queen would say to the King (whose name was also Pipsqueak. Pipsqueak Senior). 'He's got this Certain Tone Of Voice. It's most unpleasant. I can't think who he gets it from. Certainly not from me.'

To which the King would reply:

'Good gwief, Mona! Are you suggesting that the boy gets that Certain Tone Of Voice fwom me? Absolute wubbish!'

So now you know about Pipsqueak's Tone Of Voice, how it got people's backs up, and who he got it from.

It certainly got Mrs McNorty's back up. Mrs McNorty was the old woman who was employed to weed the garden, empty the rubbish bins and keep the moat free of leaves. She lived in a tumbledown hut in the castle grounds, and everyone said she was a Witch.

Here is Mrs McNorty.

She doesn't look that bad, does she? Quite a jolly old stick, really.

In fact, Mrs McNorty wasn't even a Witch any more, let alone a wicked one. She had retired from Witchcraft. There wasn't the call for it these days. Besides, she was getting too old for all that capering widdershins-around-bonfires nonsense. She much preferred gardening. She liked pottering around picking up the odd sweet wrapping and plucking out the odd nettle and scolding the odd snail and scooping the odd leaf from the moat. It was easy work, and the hours were good. She hardly ever bothered with magic any more, confining herself to the occasional anti-slug spell. Except at full moon, of course. Full moon always made her corns play up – and when her corns were playing up, she was *wicked*.

Time now to tell you what *really* happened on that fateful morning. Prince Pipsqueak woke as usual, yawned, stretched and beat his personal bedside gong. That was the signal for the servants to hop to it. Within seconds, Pipsqueak's bedroom was as busy as a railway station, except that, unlike porters, everyone wore big false smiles and bowed and tried to be helpful. A maid drew the curtains, a valet brought his slippers. A jester did a funny dance. A hairdresser brushed his hair, a minstrel wandered in and sang a flattering song, a lackey ran his bath and a flunkey squeezed his toothpaste. His crown was placed on his head. Someone blew on his dressing-gown to warm it. Just another typical morning, really.

'Lovely day, Sir,' said Grovel the butler, crawling in on his knees with a light breakfast of four kippers, two boiled eggs, four rashers of bacon and mounds of toast and marmalade served on a golden tray. 'How handsome you look first thing. Nice day for a dip, I'd say. Humbly speaking.'

'I say!' said Pipsqueak, sitting upright. 'Smart thinking, Gwovel. I shall take a wefweshing dip in the moat and pwactise my bwest stwoke. All right, gather round, you servants! Listen carefully to your orders!'

And so the servants were sent to collect the royal towel, costume, goggles, flippers and monogrammed rubber ring. That, of course, meant lots of 'I say my mans!' and 'Look, I haven't got all mornings!' and 'I am the Pwince, you knows!' and so on, so the Certain Tone Of Voice was well oiled.

At length, Pipsqueak was equipped. Off he strode, down the stairway and across the hall. The guards scurried to open the big main doors while Pipsqueak frowned and tapped his foot impatiently, complaining loudly in that awful voice of his. Then out he strode into the sunshine.

Now it was unfortunate that Mrs McNorty had chosen just that moment to take her first tea-break of the morning. There had been a full moon the night before. Her corns were killing her, and as there was no one around, she sat down at the edge of the moat, removed her boots and lowered her poor old throbbing feet into the cool water. There she sat, muttering to herself and taking big slurps out of a chipped mug. That was when Pipsqueak emerged.

Pipsqueak took one look, and then made his terrible mistake. He used That Certain Tone Of Voice on Mrs McNorty.

'I say there! Old woman! What d'you think you're doing? Stop that at once!'

'Are you talking to me, sonny?' snapped Mrs McNorty.

'I most certainly am! How dare you. You're dirtying my water!'

'I'll give you dirt,' said Mrs McNorty. 'The cheek of it!'

'Now listen here. If you don't take your disgusting feet out of my moat immediately, I shall have you awwested. I can do what I like, you know. I am the Pwince.'

'Not any more you're not,' said Mrs McNorty.

It was as simple as that. Mrs McNorty's magic might have been rusty, but she still had the touch. One moment, Pipsqueak was a Prince standing by the side of his own moat in his own castle grounds. One small, green puff of smoke later, he was a frog. Not only that, he was a frog who had been transported several miles away into a deep, muddy well which just happened to be slap in the middle of a courtyard belonging to a rival King.

Which just goes to show how careful you must be when talking to Witches.

# CHAPTER TWO

# In Which Princess Petulant Places A Large Order And Acquires A Ball

'The King of the neighbouring country had a daughter who was so beautiful that even the sun was enchanted every time he saw her. Sometimes, the Princess would play in the palace courtyard. In the middle of the courtyard was a well full of deep, clear water.'

Beautiful? Princess Petulant? Not with that nose. The only person who thought Petulant beautiful was her dad, the King – but then, he would.

King Prosperus was his name, and he ran the Kingdom next door. It was a much better kingdom than the one belonging to Pipsqueak's parents. It was bigger, and nearer the seaside. The weather was nice, so the people were more cheerful. Running a successful Kingdom is a lucrative business, and King Prosperus was incredibly, outrageously, unbelievably rich. Not only that, he was very greedy and power mad. Being a King wasn't enough for him. Oh no. He wanted to be an Emperor, because Emperors were even richer and got to boss even *more* people about. There was an election coming up soon, and King Prosperus was determined that he was going to win.

He spent a great deal of time buttering up the right people and he kissed a lot of babies. He made speeches promising extra bank holidays and a better carriage service and stiffer sentences for Witches and Wizards. My Word Is My Bond was his campaign slogan. He drove through the streets throwing gold coins and pieces of fruit-cake about, a clever ruse which was guaranteed to make people like him. In fact, his advisers informed him that the Emperorship was as good as in the bag. King Pipsqueak Senior (who also would have liked to be an Emperor) was terribly jealous about this, and the two families didn't really speak.

Here is King Prosperus.

As you can see, he has a sweet tooth. He also has a proper palace as opposed to a common castle. There are fitted carpets everywhere, and a great deal of gold paint. He has a bigger, better garden with a swimming pool. His crown is better quality. His custom-built, no-expense-spared six horse-powered golden coach requires three parking spaces. He has had to build an extension on his treasury, which groans with precious jewels, bags of gold and five-pound notes.

'Talk about ostentation,' Queen Mona would sniff. 'Have you seen that swimming pool? Vulgar, I call it. As for that coach he drives around in, talk about bad taste. He's got too much money for his own good. And have you seen that jumped-up daughter of his? Completely ruined. I've told Pipsqueak Junior to have nothing to do with her. Rude and spoilt, just like her father. If there's one thing I can't stand, it's a snob. There'll be no holding him when he's Emperor.'

'*If* he's Empewor,' Pipsqueak Senior would sneer. 'He hasn't got the job yet, wemember.'

'Don't be silly, Pipsqueak, it's as good as settled. I mean, *you're* hardly in the running. Nobody's going to vote for you, are they? What's a castle compared to a palace? And talking of palaces, when are *we* going to get one?'

It was all true. King Prosperus was a snob, and he did have far too much money. And, like most rich, doting fathers, he spent a great deal of it on his daughter, Princess Petulant. I bet you're dying to see her, aren't you?

So here she is.

See what I mean about the nose?

King Prosperus spent hours in the shops buying things for Petulant. Toys, mainly. Clothes. Unusual pets. The very latest in everything and wherever possible, in gold. You name it, Petulant had it. Going alphabetically, she had:

An aviary (well stocked with birds of prey); a billiard board (full sized); crowns by the cart-load; a drum kit; her very own elephant (full sized); five hundred and fifty-four frilly frocks; a complete set of gold-plated golf clubs; a doll's hotel; an imported igloo in biodegradable mock snow; a 9,999-piece jigsaw puzzle; Kingdomopoly (like Monopoly, except that you buy whole kingdoms); a lighthouse, a music centre, a tribe of nannies, overpriced ornaments, a python, a pet string quartet, seven rooms of her own, silk sheets, a tennis court, a stuffed unicorn, a Venetian gondola, a full-sized Snow White Musical Magical Wishing Well (genuine brick finish, toads optional), a xylophone, a yak herd and a pet zebra.

And you thought Pipsqueak was spoilt. You probably even begrudged him his expensive shoes.

This particular morning, King Prosperus was taking breakfast on the patio. He liked it there. Every time he looked up from his treacle pancakes, the rolling lawns and diamond encrusted fountains and brand-new gold-plated swimming pool reminded him how rich he was. He was planning a pleasant hour working on his extension plans. He was working out how best to extend his kingdom into an Empire. All right, so he wasn't Emperor yet – but barring any unexpected scandals, he soon would be. That Pipsqueak

Senior with his corny little castle and old fashioned moat didn't stand a chance.

King Prosperus chuckled in a self-satisfied way, and helped himself to more treacle. After lunch, maybe, he would ride around in his open-topped coach waving at peasants and throwing money and slices of Dundee cake about. Everyone who promised to vote for him would get a free Prosperus For Emperor T-shirt and a badge which said My Word Is My Bond. He was in a good mood.

'Hello, sugarplum,' he said as Princess Petulant flounced up scowling. She had only been up ten minutes, and was already bored with all her toys. Since rising, she had broken all her golf clubs, fired all her nannies and kicked her igloo to pieces. That's the sort of person she was.

'And how is my pretty popsicle this morning?' enquired King Prosperus fondly. 'Have a chocolate. Not the coffee cream, that's mine. Look! Tickets for the zoo, like I promised. My Word Is My Bond. That's my campaign slogan, you know. I think it should go down well with the voters. Are there any more toys you'd like? Any special treats? Some pretty new dresses? Sweeties? Come and give your old dad a kiss, and I'll show you the present I've bought for you.'

Yes. That really is the way he talked.

'What is it?' said Princess Petulant, tossing her hair.

'Surprise, surprise! It's a golden ball,' said King Prosperus, producing it. 'Solid gold, that is. Very exclusive. Specially made by a master goldballsman. Only the best for my daughter. Cost a King's ransom, I can tell you. Do you like it?'

'It's all right, I suppose,' said Petulant, who really didn't deserve anything because she never said thank you. 'Pity it's not bigger. Can I have a pet dolphin? There's a girl at my school who's got a pet dolphin.'

'Certainly, my little jam sponge,' said King Prosperus, patting Petulant's head. 'I'll order you one right away. Anything else I can do for my jelly baby?'

'Yes. When are you going to get that stupid Snow White Musical Magical Wishing Well taken out of my courtyard, Dad? It's babyish, and I'm bored with it. I'd like it replaced with a water splash.'

'Of course, doughnut of my dreams, of course. I'll give orders to have it removed. My Word Is My Bond. Anything else?'

He was hopelessly mad, of course.

A short time later, Petulant strolled out into the palace courtyard. She was feeling quite pleased with herself, having ordered the dolphin, the water splash, a merry-go-

round, three new party dresses, ice-skates, a
skating rink to go with them, a log cabin, a
sweet dispenser, an island, a diamond brooch
and a doll's silver banqueting set.

She crossed the courtyard, glared at the
Snow White Musical Magical Wishing Well
and gave it a spiteful kick. It attempted to
play a rusty bar or two of 'Some Day My
Prince Will Come', then wheezed into
silence.

Here is the well.

It doesn't live up to its name, does it? It is
one of King Prosperus's less successful

surprise gifts. It stands solidly in the middle of the courtyard, and is a real nuisance. It looked rather nice in the catalogue, but like most things ordered from catalogues, doesn't quite come up to expectations. As you can see, most of the tiles have dropped off, the chimes have stopped working and the handle which winches up the bucket is broken. The bucket has a hole in it. The optional toads are particularly ugly and insolent.

Right from the start, Petulant had disliked the well. What was the point of a stupid old wishing well when she got everything she wanted anyway? The moment she saw it, she wished fervently that it would disappear.

The wish wasn't granted. The well stayed firmly where it was, proving beyond all shadow of doubt that it was a total waste of time.

Apart from looking tatty and cluttering up the place, it was terribly smelly. Leaves clogged it. Moss grew on it. People spat down it. Birds flew over it and did even worse. It was choked with half-eaten elephant buns and yak droppings. Wriggly things had moved in. In short, the Snow White Musical Magical Wishing Well was a dump. The servants threw kitchen waste down there when the dustbins got too full.

Also, Petulant threw things down there when she was in a temper, so it was jam-packed with broken toys.

'Huh,' muttered Petulant. 'Wishing Well, my foot. Will I be glad to get rid of *you*.'

Idly, she began to throw the golden ball around.

# CHAPTER THREE

# In Which Pipsqueak Finds Himself Down The Well

'The well in the middle of the courtyard was the very well in which lived the enchanted Frog Prince. One day it happened that the Princess came to the courtyard to play with a golden ball. She could not catch it, and it bounced on the stones and fell with a splash into the water.'

Meanwhile, what had become of Prince Pipsqueak? If you remember, we left him at the exact moment that he got turned into a frog and cast into the very same Snow White Musical Magical Wishing Well that we've just been talking about. We should now spend a bit of time with him, and see how he's coping. After all, being turned into a frog and hurled down a strange well is a pretty major event in anyone's life. You'll be wanting to know things. Like, did it hurt?

No, it didn't. As transformations go, it was flawless. It all happened so smoothly and quickly, that Pipsqueak didn't feel a thing. All he knew was that suddenly, mysteriously, he was no longer standing by the moat using his Certain Tone of Voice on an unspeakably rude old woman. Instead, he was lying face down in some very smelly mud, while all around him swirled cold, murky, evil-smelling water.

He sat up, spat mud out of his mouth and rubbed his eyes. His first thought was that he had fallen into the moat. At this stage, you see, he didn't realize that he had been turned into a frog. He *felt* exactly the same, there weren't any mirrors around to tell him otherwise, and it's hardly the sort of thing you'd expect to happen, is it? I mean, do *you* check yourself regularly to see whether or not you've been turned into a frog? Well then.

'Gweat Scott!' thought Pipsqueak, scrambling to his feet. 'I must have fallen in the moat. How did that happen?'

He peered around. Somehow, it didn't seem like the moat. There was too much mud. The water was too dirty. And everything seemed unusually large. Massive clumps of tangled pondweed stretched high above his head. Big boulders were everywhere. It was almost as though he had shrunk.

'Funny,' thought Pipsqueak. 'I don't

wemember the moat being this filthy. And if I'm indeed underwater, how come I can bweathe? And – oh my golly! *What are all these enormous bwoken toys doing here?*'

Indeed, he appeared to be in some sort of underwater toys' graveyard. The toys, however, were huge. They looked like the playthings of some giant's child. Vast pink dolls' legs stuck up in sinister fashion from the mud. A whacking great plastic sewing machine towered above him, covered with slimy pondweed. Near by, there was a pile of torn, gigantic comics, their faded pages gently waving in the water. There was a massive broken tennis racket, and a bent, jumbo-sized diamond tiara which was big enough for him to jump through.

As his eyes adjusted themselves to the

gloom, he began to notice other things. A monstrous rusty bucket. A split sack of colossal potato peelings. A gigantic boot. A huge, leering, one-eyed teddy bear with the stuffing coming out. A pile of something utterly awful which looked suspiciously like yak droppings. Imagine the size of the yaks that produced THOSE. Pipsqueak's mind boggled. Then, it came to him.

'I must be dweaming,' thought Pipsqueak. 'That's it! I'm in the middle of a tewwible nightmare, and Gwovel will wake me up any minute. Phew. What a welief. Meanwhile, I shall stay calm.'

That was when he received the next shock. *Something cold, wet and webbed tapped him on the back!* Pipsqueak whirled round, and found himself face to face with *three toads*

*who were bigger than he was*! They squatted in a row in front of a yeuky-looking pile of pondweed. Can you imagine?

Here they are.

Urk, Arkle and Grummit. Those are their names. They are the optional toads who came with the well.

Life, as you can imagine, was rather uneventful for Urk, Arkle and Grummit, and they were quite surprised to see a strange frog suddenly appear from nowhere. However, being toads, they didn't display any emotion. They just squatted and stared and waited to see what the strange frog would do.

Much to their surprise, the strange frog burst into loud laughter. It was rather forced laughter, but it was laughter all the same.

'Ha, ha, ha!' laughed Pipsqueak, shaking his head. 'I say! What a dweam this is! Life-sized toads, eh? Whatever next. To think that my own bwain could come up with such ugly, gwotesque cweatures. All wight, that's enough of you. You didn't fwighten me, you know. I haven't woken up yet. I'm dweaming you. Go on. Clear off.'

Being a Prince, Pipsqueak, as we know, was used to giving orders. Being toads, Urk, Arkle and Grummit weren't used to taking them. Besides, they had never heard a frog use That Tone Of Voice before. They simply blinked, gaped and remained where they were. Thinking they hadn't heard, Pipsqueak tried again.

'Didn't you hear me? I command you. Even if I'm dweaming, I'm still in charge. Get out of my dweam this instant!'

'Is he talkin' to us?' asked Urk.

'Must be,' said Arkle. 'Yerp. Carn't say I like 'is Tone O' Voice. Go on, Grummit. Tell 'im to 'oppit.'

''Oppit,' said Grummit. 'This ain't no dream, mate. This 'ere's our well, see? It's a Snow White Musical Magical Wishin' Well, and we live 'ere. And you're trespassin'. Get lost.'

'Certainly not,' said Pipsqueak very

uncomfortably. Life-sized toads were one thing. Life-sized *talking* toads were another. 'I shall ignore you, of course. You're just howwible figments of my imagination.' And he folded his arms and looked the other way.

Arkle hopped up, stretched out a webbed hand, and pinched him on the back of the neck. Hard.

'No dream, froggy boy,' said Arkle.

'Ouch!' yelped Pipsqueak. 'That hurt! And what do you mean, fwoggy boy? How dare you speak to me like that. Don't you know who I am? I am the Pwince, and . . .'

He didn't get any further. Urk, Arkle and Grummit had thrown back their horny heads, and were splitting their sides.

'Oh yerp, yerp, yerp!'

''Ear that? 'Ear what 'e said?'

'A Prince, 'e says! Oh, yerp, yerp, yerp, yerp! What a joke!'

That was when Prince Pipsqueak looked down at himself for the first time.

Oh no! Horrors! He *was* a frog! A small, cold, green, slimy frog!

The terrible truth slowly dawned on him. The old woman! Of course! She must have cast a spell on him. Shakily, he put one webbed hand up to his head. Well, that was something. At least she had let him keep his crown on.

'All wight,' said Pipsqueak. 'Look, all wight, you can stop laughing. Quite obviously, and thwough no fault of my own, I have been enchanted by a Witch. I need immediate medical attention. Now, if you'd kindly show me the way out . . .'

But there was no point in continuing. Urk, Arkle and Grummit had vanished. In the short space of time it had taken Pipsqueak to establish that he was, indeed, a frog, they had simply disappeared. Gone. Vamoosed. Just like that.

'I say!' said Pipsqueak uncomfortably. 'You toads! Where are you? What's going on?'

There was a moment's silence. Then:

SPERRRLASHSHSHSHSH!

The noise was ear-splitting and it came from directly above Pipsqueak's head. He gazed upwards, and was very taken aback to see something big, round and golden hurtling towards him like a torpedo. Luckily, his brand-new frog reflexes came to his aid, and he hurled himself hastily to one side.

Shlop! The missile landed where his webbed foot had been.

Badly shaken, he watched it settle gloppily into the mud. There was a sound of tittering behind him, and Urk, Arkle and Grummit emerged from their hiding place, huge delighted grins on their faces.

'I say! You sneaks! You could have warned me!' complained Pipsqueak bitterly.

'Why?' said Urk. 'Every toad for 'imself. Never 'elp nobody. That's the toad code.'

'That'll be 'er up top again,' sniffed Grummit. 'What is it this time? A golden ball? Well, *I'm* not fetching it up for 'er.'

'Nor me,' agreed Urk. 'Never 'elp nobody.'

'Me neither,' said Arkle. 'Perhaps froggy boy 'ere would like to do the honours? 'Im an' 'er would probably get on fine. Being both *royalty* an' that. Yerp, yerp.'

Urk and Grummit sniggered, their vast stomachs going in and out like bellows.

'Who?' asked Pipsqueak. 'Who are you talking about?'

'Who d'you think? 'Er royal 'igh an' mighty. Princess Petulant of course.'

'Pwincess? Did you say *Pwincess* Petulant? King Pwospewus's daughter? But we're neighbours! I'm saved! One of my own kind! What luck!'

With a strong kick of his back legs, Pipsqueak shot up through the water. Tentacles of water weed twined around his ankles, a floating skipping rope tried to strangle him, and he nearly came a nasty cropper when trying to negotiate past a gigantic toy soldier with a very sharp wooden sword – but he was now a frog, remember, and the one thing a frog can do well is swim. His little legs and webbed feet did all the right things. It just came naturally.

Finally, triumphantly, he burst through the surface. Steep, moss-covered walls rose high all round him. An old pail dangled from a frayed rope. Far, far above was a small circle of blue sky.

'Halloooooo there!' called Pipsqueak, his voice echoing strangely. 'Mayday! Mayday! Wait wight there! I'm coming up the wope!'

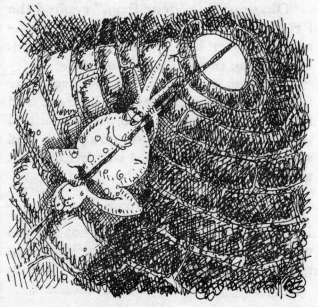

# CHAPTER FOUR

# In Which Promises Are Made

'As the golden ball sunk far out of sight, the Princess began to cry bitterly. As she wept, a voice called out, "Don't cry, Princess!" and looking up she saw an ugly frog stretching its head out of the water.

"What will you give me if I bring your ball back from the bottom of the well?" he croaked.

"Oh, anything, dear frog," replied the Princess. "My pretty dress, my diamonds, even the crown on my head. Only bring my ball back to me."

"I do not want those things," said the frog, "but if you promise to love me and let me be your playmate, to eat out of your plate, drink from your cup and sleep on your cushion, I will bring back your ball safely."

And the Princess promised.'

In fact, Petulant didn't cry. What she did was, she had a temper tantrum. Like most spoiled people, she had them frequently when things didn't go her way.

There she stood, screeching and waving her fists and kicking and shouting and generally carrying on disgracefully. She was making such a racket that she didn't even notice the small, green, anxious-looking frog with the tiny crown on its head that dragged itself up the rope and scrambled gasping on to the wall with a wild croak of 'Freedom!'

She just carried right on screaming. Pipsqueak, of course, wasn't used to being ignored.

'I say!' he shouted above the howls. 'I say! Pwincess Petulant, I pwesume? I wonder if I could have a word? I'm in a spot of bother.'

Petulant stopped in mid screech, and stared around.

'Who's that?' she said. 'Who spoke?'

'Me. Over here, on the wall.'

'Yuck,' said Petulant, spotting him. 'A yucky frog. Yuck. Go away.'

'Ah, but you're wong!' explained Pipsqueak eagerly. 'Look, I know I *look* like a fwog, but in actual fact I'm Pwince Pipsqueak fwom the kingdom next door. It's just that I've been enchanted by a Witch. It's quite simple weally.'

Even as he said it, it sounded weak.

'Pull the other leg, it's got webs on,' said Petulant rudely.

'But it's twue! I am! Look, I've got a cwown!'

'So what?' said Petulant with a shrug. 'I've got hundreds. I've got loads of dresses too, and jewels. My father's going to be an Emperor soon. Anyway, I don't believe a word of it. What's more, I don't like your Tone Of Voice.'

'Oh, for goodness sake! Where's your sense of wesponsibility? I need a hot meal, a bath, and some warm clothing. Then you must put me in your pocket and take me to the pwoper authowities. I need to contact my pawents immediately.'

'Who says I must?' said Petulant. 'What's in it for me? I don't see why I should be bossed around by a frog. You've got a nerve.

You're jealous because my dad's richer than your dad. You're after my dresses and my jewellery, aren't you? You'll be wanting to eat off my plate and drink from my cup and sleep on my cushion next. I know your sort.'

'Look, are you deaf or something? I'm *not* a fwog. I couldn't care less about your dwesses! This is a cwisis! I need help! Have mercy.'

'No thanks, never liked the stuff,' said Petulant. 'I'm not the help-giving type. You got yourself into this fix, now get yourself out of it. Unless . . .'

Her eyes narrowed craftily.

'What?' said Pipsqueak. 'Unless what?'

'Tell you what. Pop down and bring my ball up, and I might think about it. Hurry up, I haven't got all day.'

Being a Princess, Petulant was used to giving orders. Being a Prince, Pipsqueak wasn't used to taking them.

'I'm not going back down there again,' he said stiffly. 'Not for all the flies on a cowpat. Oh no! Listen to me! I'm even beginning to *talk* like a fwog now. Please, Petulant.'

'The ball,' said Petulant.

'But there are toads down there! Big, wude, common ones. How would you like to be widiculed by toads? I'm a PWINCE . . .'

'The ball,' said Petulant.

'No. It's dirty. It stinks. I won't.'

'Then stay a frog for ever,' said Petulant with a shrug. 'Why should I care? Goodbye.'

'Wait, wait! All wight! I'll get it. If I get your firm pwomise as a woyal Pwincess that you'll help me.'

'I said I'd think about it, didn't I?'

He shouldn't have trusted her, of course. But Petulant drove a hard bargain. There was nothing else for it but to fetch the golden ball. Muttering under his breath, Pipsqueak shinned down the rope, took a deep breath and once again entered the cold, murky water. Down below, Urk, Arkle and Grummit were waiting for him to provide the second act of the comedy.

'Any luck, yer royal 'ighness?' asked Grummit, helpless with wheezy giggles as Pipsqueak swam down into sight.

'Yes, if you must know,' snapped Pipsqueak. 'We woyals stick together. That's why we live in palaces and you live down wells. The Pwincess has assured me of her assistance, so yah boo sucks to you. I'm just getting the ball. As a favour.'

'Crawler,' said Urk.

'You won't get any thanks for it,' agreed Arkle. 'You expect 'elp from 'er up there? She don't know the meanin' of the word. Remember when she promised you a box of

dried mayflies for fetchin' that ruby ring up,
Urk? Never got it, did yer?'

'Did I 'eck,' growled Urk.

'Never keeps 'er word, that one,' said
Grummit sagely. 'Take my advice. Forget
it, and stay a frog. It's not a bad life, is it,
boys? Not as good as a toad's life, of course,
but not bad. Find a nice female, settle down,
'ave some tadpoles . . .'

'Look, just mind your own business,'
snarled Pipsqueak. He hopped over to the
ball and began to wrestle it out of the mud.
The toads sneered and nudged each other as
he stretched his skinny little arms as wide as
they would go, embraced the ball firmly,
and gave a mighty heave.

Out it came with a sucking plop. Pipsqueak staggered under the weight. Urk, Arkle and Grummit jeered and blew raspberries.

Pipsqueak ignored them, and kicked off. It was hard work this time. He didn't have his arms free. The weeds sucked at him and the weight of the ball was trying to pull him back down again. The skipping rope was still out to get him, and so was the soldier. However, determination triumphed, and finally, with a last desperate kick of the legs, he broke through the scummy surface.

'Have you got it?' Petulant called down. Her voice boomed eerily against the walls.

'Yes, yes, I've got it. I'm coming up.'

'Just mind you don't splash my dress.'

For the second time, Pipsqueak began to ascend the rope. Imagine trying to climb a rope with a beachball filled with cement. He almost dropped the ball several times, but at last he managed to struggle to the top.

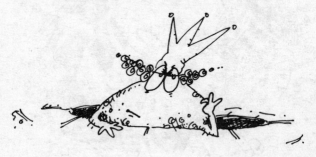

'There!' he gasped. 'Satisfied? There's your silly old ball. Now, kindly get me out of here.'

'Gracious, is that the time?' said Petulant, snatching the ball from his webbed hands. 'I thought I heard the dinner gong. Must go.'

And off she ran. Pipsqueak was flabbergasted.

# CHAPTER FIVE

# In Which King Prosperus Takes A Hand

'Later that day, as the Princess sat at dinner with the King, something came flopping up the great staircase – flip, flap, flop! – and a voice said:

> "From the deep and mossy well,
> Little playmate where I dwell,
> When you wept in grief and pain
> I brought your golden ball again."

"What is the matter, daughter?" asked the King. "There is someone knocking at the door; your rosy cheeks are quite pale."

The Princess had to tell her father how she had dropped the golden ball into the well, and how the frog had brought it up for her, and of the promises she had made to him.

Then the King frowned and said, "People who make promises must keep them. The frog shall eat from your plate, drink from your cup, and rest on

**your pillow. Open the door and let it enter."'**

It would be nice to report that Pipsqueak spoke in poetry, but of course, he didn't. Poetry? He was so miffed, he could hardly speak! You see, it had taken him the best part of the afternoon to get from the well to the palace. In the process he had twice narrowly avoided being trampled on by Petulant's elephant, who seemed to have the run of the place.

He had been clawed at by cats and dabbed at by dogs and yelled at by yaks.

He had wrestled with a python.

He had been sneered at by a zebra. He had been dive-bombed by birds of prey,

and there had been a particularly nasty moment with a lawn-mower when he was half-way across a stretch of grass.

All in all, he had had enough, and when he finally reached the palace, poetry was the last thing on his mind.

King Prosperus and Princess Petulant were just starting their supper when he appeared. If only Pipsqueak had been taller, it would have been quite a dramatic moment. He would have thrown open the door and strode in. However, being only a few inches high, he crept around it and fell over the doormat, hurting his knee quite badly. Nobody even noticed, which made it really hard to bear.

'I say!' said Pipsqueak from the doorway. His voice was choked with rage. 'Haven't you forgotten something, Pwincess Petulant? What about the meal and the hot dwink and the warm clothing, then? What about *me*? Eh? Eh?'

'Darling,' said King Prosperus, pointing a spoonful of chocolate pudding at Pipsqueak. 'There appears to be a talking frog in the room. I'm not sure I like its Tone Of Voice. Is it a friend of yours?'

'Mmm?' said Petulant, chewing unconcernedly. 'Oh, that. Certainly not. It's just Pipsqueak. You know, the Prince from that poor family who run that tacky little king-dom next door. He's been enchanted by a Witch or something, it's all terribly boring. Ignore him, Daddy.'

'Sneak!' shrieked Pipsqueak. 'Twaitor! Twickster! Sir, I accuse your daughter of tweachewy! To think I twusted her!'

'What's he talking about, creampuff?' asked King Prosperus, puzzled.

'I haven't the faintest idea. Clear off, Pip-squeak. You're putting me off my dinner. Tell him, Dad.'

'You know, I thought I recognized that Tone Of Voice,' mused King Prosperus. 'He gets it from his father. Enchanted, eh? How quaint. Can't say I've come across a case of Enchantment recently. Well, I'm afraid we can't do much about it. I won't keep you, young frog. I expect you'll be wanting to get back to your – er – mud. Now, run along, run along. Thank you for calling.' Then, in a low voice, he said:

'Honeybunny, I do wish you'd be more careful about your little playmates. It's not that I'm a snob, but we do have standards to keep up. Do you realize, his family don't even have a swimming pool? Besides, he's ruining the carpet.'

'Hah!' said Pipsqueak bitterly, flapping relentlessly up to the table. 'I was good enough to get the ball, though, wasn't I, eh?

'What ball is he talking about, cherry-pie?' asked King Prosperus.

Petulant gave a cross little stamp and threw down her spoon.

'Oh, does it really matter? That golden ball you gave me this morning. It went down the well. The frog brought it up, that's all. Big deal.'

'Yes, and in weturn, she pwomised to help me!' accused Pipsqueak, hopping up and down in a small puddle and thumping his webbed fist heavily on the King's shoe. 'What about your slogan then, King Pwospewus? My Word Is My Bond. Hah! Don't make me laugh!'

'Is this true, Pet?' asked King Prosperus. 'Did you promise this fro ... Prince Pipsqueak here that you'd help him?'

'No I didn't,' said Petulant sulkily.

'Yes you did!' insisted Pipsqueak.

'I didn't. I said I'd think about it.'

'You see? You see? That's as good as a pwomise, isn't it?' squawked Pipsqueak, all bitter accusation. 'Anyway,' he added. 'Anyway, I know when I'm not wanted. I shall find my own way home. But I tell you one thing, King Pwospewus. I'm telling. I'm going to spwead it awound that your wotten daughter can't keep her word. You wait till the town cwyers get hold of this. You'll be exposed for fwaud. We'll see what the voters have to say about *that*!'

'Now then, now then, don't let's be hasty.' King Prosperus turned quite pale. It wouldn't do to have nasty tales spread around just as the Emperorship was up for grabs. After all, he had a reputation for justice to keep up. He could just imagine the headlines:

# SENSATION! TOP KING EXPOSED BY FROG

Sources revealed today that King 'My Word Is My Bond' Prosperus, hot favourite in the race for the Emperorship, is being sued for breach of promise by a frog claiming to be Prince Pipsqueak Junior, son of King Pipsqueak Senior. The frog's heart-broken father is quoted as saying, 'Pipsqueak was deserted in his hour of need. I'll never forgive Pwospewus for not helping our boy. He doesn't deserve to be Empewor. I do.' Friends of the Frog are also considering bringing a cruelty charge. When challenged, King Prosperus replied, 'It wasn't me, it was my daughter.'

It didn't sound good. It certainly wouldn't put him in a good light with the voters. Whereas 'SENSATION! TOP KING RESCUES FROG!' would. In fact, it wouldn't do him any harm at all. Now, there was a thought. Maybe he could turn the situation to his own advantage and come out looking like a hero.

King Prosperus made a decision. He suddenly became very stern with Petulant, and fawningly friendly towards Pipsqueak.

'Prince Pipsqueak has a point, daughter. One good turn deserves another. It is our duty to help this poor, unfortunate young fr – fellow. Our Word Is Our Bond, remember? Now then, young Pipsqueak, have you eaten? What about a spot of supper? Petulant, draw up a chair for our guest.'

'Oh, but, Dad . . .'

'*Do as I say!* Pipsqueak, is there anything you particularly fancy? I can recommend the salad. I'm afraid the chocolate pudding's all gone. Can I order you a side plate of – er – flies or anything?'

'No thank you,' said Pipsqueak stiffly. 'Salad will do just fine. I'll use your plate, Petulant. Kindly lift me up on the table and pass the mayonnaise.'

'Get lost,' snarled Petulant. 'No greasy old frog's eating off my plate.'

'Petulant! Where are your manners? Do as he asks this minute!' instructed King Prosperus.

'Oh, but, Dad . . .'

'You heard.'

Face red with fury, Petulant stooped down, snatched up Pipsqueak and roughly dumped him on the table.

'Gently, gently. You'll bruise our young guest. Now, make yourself at home, my dear fro – friend. Offer Prince Pipsqueak a drink, Petulant, and pass him a serviette to sit on. It'll be more comfortable for him, besides protecting the cloth. Now then, young Pipsqueak, do tell me, how is your delightful mother? And your father, Pipsqueak Senior? Do they still live in that charming little castle? I really must drop round and see them sometime.'

'I think they'll pwobably be a bit worried about me by now,' said Pipsqueak, yawning. He had had a tough day, and was beginning to feel terribly tired.

'Of course, of course. I shall contact them immediately. How do you find the salad? Find Pipsqueak a spoon, Pet, he'll do himself a terrible injury with that fork. Now, do tell me all about this Enchantment business. I must admit I'm rather fascinated . . .'

But Pipsqueak, worn out by his terrifying

ordeal, had keeled over into the salad bowl, and was fast asleep.

'I think he can be cleared away now, Petulant,' said King Prosperus coldly. 'Take him to the bathroom, and make him comfortable in the sink. Not on my flannel, if you please. If he wakes, soft-soap him. Smile at him. Talk to him. Give him a kiss. Tell him being a frog suits him. Whatever he wants, get it.'

'But, DAD . . .'

'No arguments! Do you realize, this could cost me the Emperorship? However, despite your foolishness, I think I can wriggle out of this and, hopefully, come up smelling of roses. No thanks to you. You can forget the dolphin. Perhaps that will make you think twice about making rash promises to frogs in future. I must send a messenger to the frog's parents, and order the bells to be rung and reporters to be present and so on. Off you go – and remember, BE NICE TO HIM.'

# CHAPTER SIX

# In Which Pipsqueak
Is Sadly Missed

'Meanwhile, the handsome Prince's
mother and father mourned the loss of
their son.'

True. But that one little sentence barely de-
scribes the incredible fuss that was made
back at the castle when it was discovered
that Pipsqueak was missing. The grounds
were searched. The moat was drained. All
the servants were cross-examined, including
Mrs McNorty, who denied all knowledge.
When interviewed, she kept burying her face
in a handkerchief to hide her giggles.

Mrs McNorty was enjoying all the drama.
It was a long time since she had been that
wicked, and it went to her head. She had, in
fact, been watching Pipsqueak's adventures
with the aid of her crystal ball. She found it
so entertaining, she even invited a couple of
old cronies over to watch with her. They all
agreed it was better than the pictures.

'Aren't I naughty?' said Mrs McNorty,
wiping her eyes. 'I'll change him back soon,
of course. Just as soon as I'm sure he's learnt

his lesson. Hey! Come and watch this bit, with the toads!'

'I'm sure that old woman knows more than she says she does, you know, Pipsqueak,' fretted Queen Mona. 'Didn't you notice? She kept burying her face in a disgraceful old hanky. I'm sure she was laughing. Perhaps she's a Witch.'

'Nonsense, deawest. You're overwought,' said King Pipsqueak Senior, patting her shoulder.

'But you hear all these stories about enchanted Princes, don't you? I mean, it's not uncommon. And darling Pipsqueak Junior does have a way of getting people's backs up . . .'

'But he's not handsome,' pointed out King

Pipsqueak Senior. 'They're usually hand-some, aren't they? The ones that get en-chanted.'

'I suppose so,' sniffed Queen Mona, re-cognizing the truth of this. 'Oh, Pipsqueak! Where *are* you?'

'I'm here,' said King Pipsqueak.

'Not you, stupid. I meant our son, of course!'

'Ah,' said King Pipsqueak. 'Yes, of course. I see what you mean. Bear up, dear. I'm sure we'll get some news soon. In fact, there's a messenger galloping up the fwont path wight now. I'll go and see what he wants.'

The Queen sat and snivelled and bit her finger-nails while Pipsqueak Senior was deal-ing with the messenger. When he came back in, his face was grave.

'Well?' said the Queen.

'Good news. He's been found.'

'Oh, but Pipsqueak, that's wonderful!' cried Queen Mona. 'Where is he? Where is my boy?'

'Ah. Yes. Well, the bad news is . . . ahem . . . he's a fwog.'

'I beg your pardon?' said the Queen.

'He's a fwog. Now, stay calm, Mona, and stop biting the wallpaper. He's turned up in a well in King Pwospewus's courtyard of all places. It seems you were wight, dear. He has been enchanted. But don't wowwy, he's quite safe. All we have to do is go and pick him up. Er – how do you feel about picking up fwogs, Mona?'

'I shan't mind if it truly is my Pipsqueak,' said Queen Mona stoutly. 'A mother's love can move mountains. And I shall wear gloves, of course. Oh, my poor, poor darling, changed into a frog and cast down a well. I bet it's a vulgar one too if it belongs to Prosperus. Oh dear! Pipsqueak! Do you think the spell will wear off?'

'Oh, sure to,' said King Pipsqueak uncertainly. 'They always do eventually. Look,

pop your cwown on, and I'll bwing the coach wound. We'll go and collect him. Oh, bother the boy. Can you imagine the mileage Pwospewus will get out of this? I'll never be Empewor now.'

'Never mind the Emperorship! What about sleeping arrangements?' wailed Queen Mona, wringing her hands. 'Will he want his own room, or should I clear out the aquarium or something? Wait a minute, he's sure to be hungry, I must pack up a snack. What do frogs eat? Oh, Pipsqueak, I'm not sure I can handle this!'

Pipsqueak Senior wasn't too sure about handling frogs either.

# CHAPTER SEVEN

# In Which Pipsqueak
# Gets Dunked Again

'The Princess wept. She had had more than she could bear. Not only had the frog shared her supper, but now he was to sleep in her very own, pretty room.

Obediently, she placed the frog on a silken pillow and carried him to her bedchamber. Once there, she laid him on her white coverlet.

"One last request, Princess," begged the frog. "A kiss. One kiss from your red lips."

The Princess quailed, but, remembering her father's words, she gently lifted the frog and pressed her lips to his cold skin.'

You will know enough of everyone concerned by now to know that this was *not* the way it happened. For 'The Princess wept', substitute 'The Princess sulked'. For 'silken pillow', substitute 'bowl of salad'. For 'bedchamber', substitute 'bathroom'. For 'pressed her lips to his cold skin', substitute 'cold-bloodedly attempted to flush him down the toilet'.

Yes. Unbelievable though it may seem, that's what happened.

Petulant, you see, was furious. It was the first time in her life that she'd been made to do something she didn't want to do, and believe me, it showed.

She argued. She shouted and stamped. She tried to trip up the messenger who was sent to take the good news. She threw things. But, for once, she didn't get her own way. King Prosperus could not be moved, and finally Petulant had to give in.

Fuming, she snatched up the bowl of salad containing the sleeping Pipsqueak and slammed out of the room. Pipsqueak stirred, mumbled something, and snuggled up to a chunk of cucumber. Muttering under her breath, Petulant marched down the corridor and into the bathroom.

'What's happening?' said Pipsqueak sleepily as he was rudely plucked from his bed and held upside-down by one foot. 'Is that you, Gwovel? Is the nightmare over? Is it morning?'

'What's happening is, I'm getting rid of you,' said Petulant, grimly lifting the toilet lid. 'You've been nothing but trouble. Goodbye for ever.'

'I say! Steady on! You wouldn't dare!' protested the dangling Pipsqueak.

'Wouldn't I just?'

And Petulant let go.

It's a cruel world. For the third time that day, Pipsqueak was plunged into cold water against his will.

Plonk!

Splosh!

He was up to his neck in it.

It wasn't a nice place to be. The well was bad enough, but even that was preferable to a toilet. Even one with a posh golden seat and tassles on the chain. Being an undeniably superior toilet, this one deserves a proper picture.

And here it is.

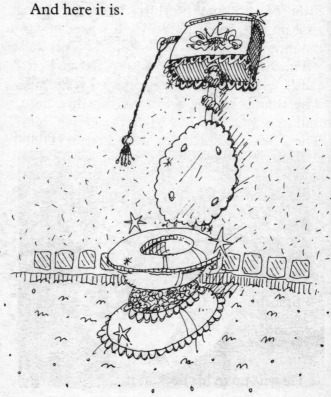

As toilets go, it's a nice one. But it's still a toilet, and a toilet is a toilet however hard you may try to disguise the fact. And Pipsqueak knows it. You can't help feeling a bit sorry for him.

Keeping his mouth firmly closed, he trod water and tried not to panic. To one side yawned an unsavoury black hole. And Pipsqueak didn't fancy it down there. Not one little bit. Smooth, white slippery slopes rose up all around him. They looked insurmountable.

Pipsqueak looked up. High above, Petulant's grinning face peered down at him. The thumb of one hand was on her nose, and she was wiggling her fingers at him. The other hand held the tassled chain.

'All wight,' croaked Pipsqueak. His voice bounced echoing off the porcelain. 'Enough's enough. Joke over. You've gone too far now.'

'Not as far as you're going,' said Petulant with a nasty laugh and slammed the lid down. Instant darkness, and a sense of impending doom.

'Look. This isn't funny, Petulant.'

'Yes it is,' said Petulant. Her voice sounded muffled and far away. 'Where's your sense of adventure?'

'Look, my pawents will be here any minute. How are you going to explain this?'

'Easy. I'll say you hopped off somewhere.'

'Fiend!' gasped Pipsqueak, bobbing around desperately. 'Barbarian!'

'Not at all,' said Petulant airily. 'I'm just your average fairy-tale Princess. Most of us are awful. Bye bye.'

And she pulled the chain.

There was a terrible gushing, roaring noise and a torrent of water came crashing down. Imagine standing directly beneath the Niagara Falls. That's how it feels to be a frog in a flushing toilet. The force of the deluge knocked him off balance, and he found himself swirling around underwater, hopelessly out of control.

He closed his eyes. He didn't want to look. *He knew he was being sucked towards the hole!*

# CHAPTER EIGHT

# In Which Pipsqueak Is Rescued

'At the touch of her lips, he was changed from an ugly frog back into the handsome young Prince and he cried, "Oh Princess, you have broken the Witch's spell and I am myself again. Now you shall be my wife, for you are the prettiest Princess in the world and I have loved you from the first moment I saw you!"

The Princess and the Prince became husband and wife, and they lived happily ever after.'

Well! Can you *believe* this? Are we seriously expected to believe that after all Pipsqueak had been through, he would propose marriage? Or that, if he did, Petulant would accept him? Hardly. This is what really happened:

As Pipsqueak was on the point of being flushed away, several things happened elsewhere.

First of all, his parents arrived at the palace. Queen Mona, face awash with tears and crown askew, leapt from the coach, pushed her way through the crowds of reporters, ran up the steps and began hammering madly at the palace doors demanding the return of her son. King Pipsqueak Senior followed sheepishly behind, muttering 'No Comment' and carrying a small goldfish bowl and an alternative packed lunch of ants' eggs and ham sandwiches.

King Prosperus stood in the doorway, every inch the hero.

'Pipsqueak, old man! How very nice to see you. I hear you're running for the Emperorship. May the best King win, eh? And Mona, my dear, how very charming you look. Yes, your son is quite safe. My daughter has made him comfortable. Not at all, not at all, glad to be of service. Shocking business, the lad being turned into a frog. Good thing he came to me. Of course, I said I'd help right away. Did you get that, you reporters? Now, if you'd like to step this way, I'll take you straight to him . . .'

Back at the castle, the servants were preparing a large 'Welcome Home' banner for Pipsqueak. They were drawing frogs all over it, and killing themselves laughing.

At the same time, some men arrived to take the Snow White Musical Magical Wishing Well away. You'll be pleased to know that Urk, Arkle and Grummit escaped, and made a new life for themselves in King Prosperus's swimming pool.

Lastly – luckily – Mrs McNorty came back from making a cup of tea, and peered into her crystal ball.

'Oh lawks!' said Mrs McNorty. 'I'd better turn him back now. Sorry, girls, the fun's over. I'll say a quick reversing spell. That should do the trick.'

And she did. And it did. It was as simple as that.

One minute, Pipsqueak was an enchanted frog being sucked against his wishes down a hole in a toilet bowl. One large, yellow explosion later, he was a full-sized Prince. Still not handsome, but a Prince all right.

What a relief.

Petulant gnashed her teeth in frustration as the yellowish smoke cleared and the lid of the toilet slowly began to rise. The crown appeared first, followed by head, then shoulders, then the rest of him. Finally, Pipsqueak stepped out of the bowl. He was soaking wet but quite intact, even down to the expensive shoes (which, of course, were quite ruined).

'Hah!' said Pipsqueak, his voice ringing with triumph. 'Foiled, Petulant! It seems that the spell has worn off, and I am myself again. What d'you have to say to that, eh?'

'Get lost,' snarled Petulant with a withering sneer. 'And don't go thinking you can marry me either. Quite frankly, I preferred you as a frog.'

'*Mawwy* you?' screeched Pipsqueak. 'Mawwy *you*? I'd sooner mawwy a – a – a – slug! A snake! A . . . I'm going to wing your neck!' And he squelched towards her.

Just then, there was the sound of distant voices.

'Where is he? Where's my boy?' (Queen Mona.)

'I can assure you, madam, he's being well looked after in the bathroom . . .' (Prosperus.)

'The bathroom! They've got him in the bathroom, Pipsqueak!'

Running footsteps, followed by a frantic rattling at the door.

'Pipsqueak Junior!' sobbed Queen Mona. 'Mum's here, darling. We've come to take you home. I've brought some sandwiches! I still love you, even if you are a frog!'

The door burst open, and in they all rushed. Queen Mona, King Pipsqueak Senior, King Prosperus, assorted servants and at least a dozen reporters.

'Where is he? Where's the frog?' shouted the reporters, cameras at the ready and pencils poised.

'Here! It's me. At least, I was until a minute ago, then there was a flash, and I'm myself again. Oh, Mummy! Thank goodness you're here. She twied to flush me away!'

The reporters looked disappointed at having missed the best bit.

'Ha, ha,' laughed King Prosperus. 'Ha, ha, ha. Just his little joke. In fact, we've been taking great care of him . . .'

'His shoes!' hissed Queen Mona. 'Look at his beautiful, expensive shoes! They're soaking! Are you calling my son a liar, King Prosperus? If my son says your daughter tried to flush him down the toilet, that's what happened. We tell the truth in our family.'

'Sneak!' hissed Princess Petulant un-

pleasantly as the reporters scribbled away. There then followed the sort of scene that everyone dreads. Everyone was screaming and making threats. It was all getting horribly out of hand. It went a bit like this:

Queen Mona: 'Did you hear that? Did you hear that, everyone? She tried to flush my son down the toilet! Pipsqueak, are you a king or a mouse? Do something!'

King Prosperus: 'My dear madam, I can assure you your son is mistaken. My daughter never intended anything of the kind, did you, Pet?'

| | |
|---|---|
| Petulant: | 'Yes I did. Best place for him.' |
| Reporter: | 'Can I quote you on that, your Royal Highness?' |
| King Pipsqueak: | 'Right, Pwosperus, I've just about had enough of you. Put up your fists, you fat swankpot. Somebody hold this goldfish bowl and let me get at him!' |

Luckily, Mrs McNorty took a hand. The scene in the crystal ball was so disgraceful that she had to do something. What she did was, she separated them. It happened so quickly, that the warring factions found themselves shouting at thin air. Pipsqueak and his parents were whisked back to their own castle, to be greeted by cheering servants singing a mocking chorus of 'For he's a jolly good frog prince'.

Prosperus and Petulant were left with a great deal of explaining to do.

But the story didn't quite end there. You'll want to know the outcome, I'm sure. This is what happened. There is good news and bad news.

Bad news for King Prosperus. He wasn't elected as Emperor. Although he paid out a fortune in hush money, the story got out, and he lost all credibility. People laughed at his motto and the voters deserted him in droves. In the end, he had to sell his palace and look for somewhere smaller.

Bad news for Petulant. She no longer got all those presents. In fact, her pocket money was stopped, and she was sent off to A School For Young Princesses, where everyone behaved as badly as she did and gave her a hard time because she was a new girl.

Good news for King Pipsqueak Senior. Against all odds, he got the Emperorship. He wasn't particularly good at it, but then he wasn't particularly bad either, as long as he didn't try to make speeches. Oh, and he bought King Prosperus's palace, which of course was . . .

Good news for Queen Mona. She became Empress, and was able to buy an entire new wardrobe and live in a palace, which was what she always wanted.

Bad news for Mrs McNorty. She got fired. However, she got herself re-employed immediately by disguising herself as a rosy-cheeked peasant woman. Her job was to keep the swimming pool free from leaves at the new palace.

Bad news for Pipsqueak, I'm afraid. One morning, shortly after they had moved, Pipsqueak decided to sample the swimming pool. To his disgust, what should he find but a rosy-cheeked peasant woman dangling her legs in the water and slurping from an old cup.

'I say!' said Pipsqueak, using A Certain Tone Of Voice. 'I say! You there! What do you think you're doing? Get your disgusting feet out of my water this minute!'

It's a pity it was a full moon. Some people never learn.

# READ MORE IN PUFFIN

For children of all ages, Puffin represents quality and variety – the very best in publishing today around the world.

For complete information about books available from Puffin and Penguin – and how to order them, contact us at the appropriate address below. Please note that for copyright reasons the selection of books varies from country to country.

**On the worldwide web**: www.puffin.co.uk

**In the United Kingdom**: Please write to *Dept. EP, Penguin Books Ltd, Bath Road, Harmondsworth, West Drayton, Middlesex UB7 ODA*

**In the United States**: Please write to *Consumer Sales, Penguin USA, P.O. Box 999, Dept. 17109, Bergenfield, New Jersey 07621-0120.* VISA and MasterCard holders call 1-800-253-6476 to order Penguin titles

**In Canada**: Please write to *Penguin Books Canada Ltd, 10 Alcorn Avenue, Suite 300, Toronto, Ontario M4V 3B2*

**In Australia**: Please write to *Penguin Books Australia Ltd, P.O. Box 257, Ringwood, Victoria 3134*

**In New Zealand**: Please write to *Penguin Books (NZ) Ltd, Private Bag 102902, North Shore Mail Centre, Auckland 10*

**In India**: Please write to *Penguin Books India Pvt Ltd, 706 Eros Apartments, 56 Nehru Place, New Delhi 110 019*

**In the Netherlands**: Please write to *Penguin Books Netherlands bv, Postbus 3507, NL-1001 AH Amsterdam*

**In Germany**: Please write to *Penguin Books Deutschland GmbH, Metzlerstrasse 26, 60594 Frankfurt am Main*

**In Spain**: Please write to *Penguin Books S. A., Bravo Murillo 19, 1° B, 28015 Madrid*

**In Italy**: Please write to *Penguin Italia s.r.l., Via Felice Casati 20, I–20124 Milano*

**In France**: Please write to *Penguin France S. A., 17 rue Lejeune, F–31000 Toulouse*

**In Japan**: Please write to *Penguin Books Japan, Ishikiribashi Building, 2–5–4, Suido, Bunkyo-ku, Tokyo 112*

**In South Africa**: Please write to *Longman Penguin Southern Africa (Pty) Ltd, Private Bag X08, Bertsham 2013*